MW00882130

MINECRAFT
STONESWORD SAGA

THE END OF THE OVERWORLD!

This is a work of fiction. Names, characters, places, and incidents either are the product of the author's imagination or are used fictitiously. Any resemblance to actual persons, living or dead, events, or locales is entirely coincidental.

© 2024 Mojang AB. All Rights Reserved. Minecraft, the Minecraft logo, the Mojang Studios logo and the Creeper logo are trademarks of the Microsoft group of companies.

Published in the United States by Random House Children's Books, a division of Penguin Random House LLC, 1745 Broadway, New York, NY 10019, and in Canada by Penguin Random House Canada Limited, Toronto. Random House and the colophon are registered trademarks of Penguin Random House LLC.

rhcbooks.com
minecraft.net

Library of Congress Cataloging-in-Publication Data is available upon request.
ISBN 978-0-593-56294-9 (trade)—ISBN 978-0-593-56295-6 (lib. bdg.)—
ISBN 978-0-593-56296-3 (ebook)

Cover design by Diane Choi

Printed in the United States of America
3rd Printing

THE END OF THE OVERWORLD!

By Nick Eliopulos

Illustrated by Alan Batson and Chris Hill

Random House 🏠 New York

MORGAN

ASH

HARPER

PO

JODI

THEO

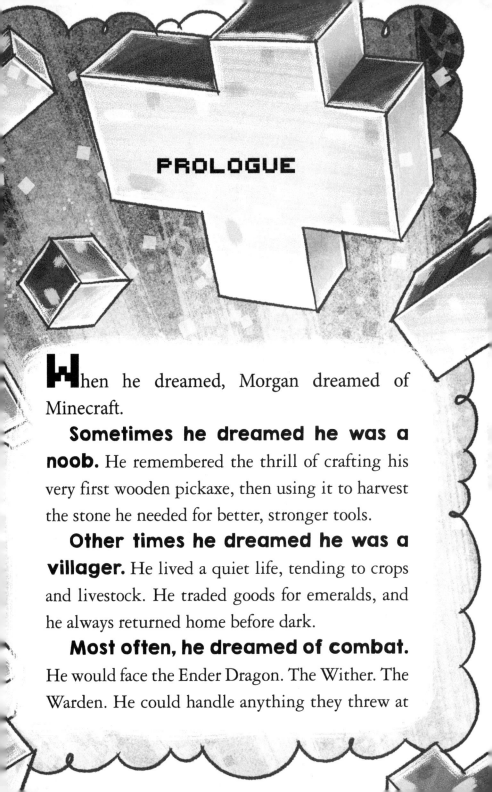

PROLOGUE

Hhen he dreamed, Morgan dreamed of Minecraft.

Sometimes he dreamed he was a noob. He remembered the thrill of crafting his very first wooden pickaxe, then using it to harvest the stone he needed for better, stronger tools.

Other times he dreamed he was a villager. He lived a quiet life, tending to crops and livestock. He traded goods for emeralds, and he always returned home before dark.

Most often, he dreamed of combat. He would face the Ender Dragon. The Wither. The Warden. He could handle anything they threw at him. (Even the time he dreamed that the Ender Dragon had given him a pop quiz in chemistry. It had spoken in Doc's voice. That was weird!)

Tonight, Morgan dreamed a nightmare vision of a Minecraft that had been broken into pieces. The sky was a starless void. The horizon was a lifeless sea of bedrock. Morgan was standing on a tiny patchwork island: a bit of grass, some rocky rubble, a jungle tree, and a few mushrooms. That was all that was left of the game Morgan had loved with all his heart.

It seemed as if Minecraft was dying—breaking down into a digital abyss. **And unless he wanted to go down with it, Morgan had to escape.**

Luckily, he had planned for this. He had obsidian in his inventory. With the speed of a master builder, he constructed a portal on the grass. **That portal, he knew, was his ticket to safety.**

But he didn't have any way to turn it on.

Morgan cursed himself for forgetting to craft

the flint and steel he needed to light the portal and make his escape. He would have to mine for the materials. It was his only hope.

Morgan brought his pickaxe down hard.

Too hard.

The force was too great for the little island. **It shattered like glass.** The final fragment of the Overworld had been destroyed by Morgan's own carelessness.

And there was no more solid ground for him to stand on.

Morgan fell into the void, screaming.

He was still screaming when he awoke in his bed.

He was safe. But was Minecraft?

Chapter 1

IT WAS A DARK AND STORMY AFTERNOON! SO OBVIOUSLY AN OMINOUS WARNING OF THINGS TO COME!

A storm was raging outside Woodsword Middle School, but Morgan Mercado barely noticed.

Because a storm of a different kind was raging inside his heart.

Morgan loved Minecraft. If he wasn't playing the game, he was often thinking about it and discussing it with his friends. Every birthday, he had a cake in the shape of a different Minecraft mob. His school folders and notebook were covered with Minecraft stickers and sketches. He had dressed as an Enderman for Halloween two years in a row!

And now the game he loved was in trouble. **How could Morgan let anything distract him from that?**

The bell rang, signaling that school was over for the day. **But Morgan's work was just beginning.** He leapt out of his chair, threw his backpack over his shoulder, and hurried past rows of desks and a brightly decorated bulletin board. He was the first student out the door.

His sister, Jodi, was waiting for him at his locker. She had a smudge of paint on her nose and more paint stains on her fingertips. It looked like she'd just come from art class.

"I thought math was your last class of the day," said Morgan.

"It is," Jodi replied. "I thought it would be a great idea to use watercolor paints on my math test." She wiggled her paint-stained fingers. **"I was right!"**

Morgan shoved his textbooks into his locker and zipped his backpack. "Do you need to wash up?"

"There's no time," Jodi said. **"We have to get to the library as soon as we can.** We have to get *into Minecraft* as soon as we can."

Morgan grinned. He couldn't agree more.

The siblings hurried down the hallway. Students were gathering for after-school activities. They saw a group of kids in neckerchiefs and badge-bedecked sashes. **Those were the Wildling Scouts.** Their friend Ash Kapoor had been in this scouting troop before she moved away. Morgan and Jodi recognized a few of them and smiled hello as they passed.

The next cluster of kids were members of Woodsword's student government. **Morgan's best friend, Po Chen, was one of them.**

Po saw them and waved. Then he turned to Shelly Silver, the class president. "Sorry, Shelly," he said. "I've got to head to the library with Morgan and Jodi."

"**No problem,**" said Shelly. "I'll let you know what you miss. Maybe I'll drop in and join you guys for Minecraft sometime!"

"**You play Minecraft?**" Morgan asked.

"Doesn't everybody?" said Shelly, and she turned to enter a nearby classroom.

Po rolled his wheelchair alongside Morgan and Jodi. "Perfect timing," he told them.

"Are you sure you can miss the meeting?" asked Jodi.

"I'm in a lot of clubs," Po reminded her. "Student government, basketball, and theater. But with what's going on in Minecraft, we need to tackle that first. You know that!"

Morgan grinned. His friends were the best.

And two more of those friends were just ahead.

"Today's the day," said Theo Grayson. **"We have to fix the Fault before it's too late."**

"And more important, we have to save the Evoker King," said Harper. "The EK is made up of game code. If the game falls apart, he falls apart with it."

They weren't saying anything that Morgan didn't agree with.

The Evoker King was an artificial intelligence—a digital being—who existed inside their current Minecraft campaign. But the Evoker King had split up into six separate mobs at the same time that a "Fault" of broken pixels had appeared in the Minecraft sky. **That Fault had grown to swallow nearly the entire Overworld.** But Morgan and his friends hoped that putting the Evoker King back together would fix the game, too.

It was the best idea they had. And they were close. They'd already gathered five of the six "Evoker Spawn." Only one of the strange mobs remained.

They could do this. They could restore the Evoker King and reverse the damage caused by the Fault. **They could win the day!**

But first they had to cross the street. The computer that hosted their Minecraft game was in the Excalibur County Library and Media Center, aka **Stonesword Library**, immediately across from their school. And so were the special VR goggles that allowed them to actually project themselves into the game.

Morgan pushed open the front doors of the

school. To his surprise, a strong wind grabbed the door and slammed it open with a loud *KLANG!* He could see the library just ahead, through heavy sheets of rain. **Thunder rumbled overhead.**

"I forgot my umbrella," said Harper.

"I have one," said Theo. "But it's not big enough for all of us."

"We're getting wet, then," said Po.

"Oh, good," said Jodi. "I could use the wash!"

"On three, everybody," said Morgan. "One. Two. Three!"

Morgan charged ahead into the storm. The crossing guard helped them cross the street, holding up a small stop sign to stop road traffic. Morgan found himself wishing the sign would work on the rain and wind. Water was seeping down the back of his shirt and into his shoes. It was everywhere!

Morgan was surprised to see Mr. Mallory, the library's media specialist, standing outside the front entrance. He was wearing a poncho and standing beneath an awning, but neither was doing a very good job of keeping him dry. He cradled the library's hamster, Duchess Dimples, to his chest. **It looked like he'd been crying.** But that was probably just the rain wetting his cheeks, right?

"Mr. Mallory?" said Harper. **"Is everything okay?"**

Mr. Mallory blinked, then finally seemed to realize they were there.

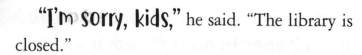

"**I'm sorry, kids,**" he said. "The library is closed."

"But why?" said Theo. "It's only three o'clock!"

"You don't understand," said Mr. Mallory. "I mean the library is closed *indefinitely*. The roof collapsed. The building is flooding. **It's a disaster in there!**"

Morgan's eyes went wide. "The tech equipment!" he said. "Is it okay?"

Mr. Mallory frowned. **He pulled an object from beneath his poncho.** It was dripping with water.

"Th-that's one of the VR headsets we use for Minecraft," Morgan said.

"Not anymore," said Mr. Mallory. "I'm sorry, kids, but all five headsets were caught in the flood. It looks like they got the worst of it. **They're drenched!**"

Chapter 2

WATER: BANE OF BOOKS! ENEMY OF ELECTRONICS! HONESTLY, WHY DO WE EVEN KEEP WATER AROUND?

Harper tossed and turned all night long. She couldn't stop thinking about the damaged library. As she usually did when she learned about a big problem, she wished desperately that she could fix it.

Harper was an amateur scientist. And she believed that science, *good* science, was all about solving problems.

But it was too late to prevent the damage to the library. Was it also too late to save their Minecraft campaign?

As she lay awake, she reminded herself that Minecraft itself wasn't

going away. She and her friends would always be able to play their favorite game. They could generate a new world from scratch and work together to gather the materials they'd lost. **They could craft all their favorite gear, weapons, items, potions, and so on.** It was fun to occasionally start over from the beginning.

But the version of the game she'd shared with Morgan, Jodi, and the others was special. And not just because of the experimental VR goggles that had transported them into the game. **What had really made their game unique was the Evoker King.** As an evolving, self-aware artificial intelligence, the Evoker King was truly one of a kind. She thought of him as a friend. And because he was made of programming, he was stuck in that world. He was *part* of that world.

If that world was destroyed, **her friend would be destroyed with it.**

How was Harper supposed to get any sleep with thoughts like that on her mind?

The next day, Harper could tell she wasn't the only one who'd had trouble sleeping. Jodi had bags under her eyes, and **Theo yawned** as he greeted her in front of the school.

But Morgan looked as awake and intense as Harper had ever seen him.

"There must be something we can do," he said. "Harper, Theo, do you two have any ideas?"

They were all gathered in Woodsword's gym before the first bell. Usually, they would meet on the front lawn, beneath their favorite tree. **But the storm was still raging.** The wind rattled the doors, as if trying to find its way inside.

"**Hey!**" said Po. "Why are you asking Harper and Theo for ideas? We're all equally smart on this team."

"You're right, Po," said Morgan. "I'm sorry. Did you have an idea?"

Po grinned. He waggled his fingers as if casting a magic spell. "**Time travel,**" he said.

Morgan sighed, and Jodi patted Po on the head. "We'll work on it," she promised.

"There's not much we can do without the VR goggles," Theo said, and he yawned again. "The specific instance of Minecraft that we've been playing . . . or visiting . . . is keyed to those devices. **The world itself is hosted on a library computer, but without the goggles, we have no way of accessing it.**"

Harper nodded in agreement with Theo. She saw the desperate hope in Morgan's eyes. He wasn't ready to give up on the Evoker King. She admired that about him. But she couldn't think of a single encouraging thing to say. And she saw the hope in Morgan's eyes start to fade away.

"**I can see you're all upset about the**

library," said a voice. "I am, too."

Harper turned, and at first, she thought she was seeing a ghost. A tall figure loomed before them, dressed all in black, its face obscured by a shadowy veil. But there was no disguising the frizzy red curls that belonged to their homeroom teacher.

"Ms. Minerva!" said Harper. "Are you going to a funeral?"

"In a manner of speaking," said the teacher. "I'm mourning the destruction of the library. It's a terrible loss for our community, isn't it? **All those poor, defenseless books, lost to the ravages of nature.** It's almost Shakespearean!"

"Oh, Minerva, must you be so dramatic?" said another voice—one that Harper recognized instantly. **Her favorite teacher, Doc Culpepper, approached them with a skip in her step.** "You know what I always say: every setback is an opportunity for invention. And I think we can all agree that what the library needed all along was a state-of-the-art force field!"

Harper couldn't see Ms. Minerva's expression with the veil in place, but she could sense her rolling her eyes. "Even a force field lets light through," Ms. Minerva said. **"And light can damage books, too, given enough time."**

"Challenge accepted!" said Doc. "If you can get me funding, I will invent a barrier that will block both rain *and* light."

"But . . . that's just a roof, isn't it?" said Theo.

Doc narrowed her eyes. **"Then I will make a**

state-of-the-art roof. With science!"

"Why are the teachers hanging out with us?" Po whispered. "It's weird, right?"

Harper elbowed him. It was her way of saying *Shush!*

"**Look there,**" said Doc. "Is that Mr. Mallory?"

Harper saw immediately that Doc was right. The media specialist was coming in from the rain. Doc and Ms. Minerva waved him over.

"Are you here to check on Duchess Dimples?" asked Ms. Minerva. "She's settling in just fine."

"**Or are you here to request a force field?**" asked Doc. "Because I'm still puzzling out an appropriate power source."

Mr. Mallory raised his eyebrow. "Nothing like that," he answered. "I'm here to greet some student volunteers. A troop of Wildling Scouts has volunteered to help us

with all the cleanup."

"It will be heartbreaking," said Ms. Minerva. "Sifting through the ruin of the library."

Mr. Mallory shook his head. "The flooding made a mess, and it destroyed some of our physical collection. **But a library is more than just a building.** I can continue to serve the community while the roof is being repaired and books are being replaced." He smiled. "And since many of our materials are available online, you'll still be able to access our collection. I just turned the computers on this morning."

"And the Wildling Scouts are going to help you?" asked Theo. "Won't they miss class?"

"Aw, no fair," said Po. "That's, like, the *one* club I'm not in."

"The Wildling volunteers are coming from a neighboring town, actually," said Mr. Mallory. "Their school calendar is different from Woodsword's. **They're on break this week. Ah! Here they are now."**

They all peered out the window. Through the rain, Harper saw a school bus pull up to the curb. Its door opened, and a stream of Wildling Scouts stepped out, holding their umbrellas high.

One of them was familiar.

"Everybody, look! It's Ash!" cried Harper. **"Ash is here!"**

Chapter 3

WELCOME BACK, ASH! I HOPE YOU LIKE WHAT WE'VE DONE WITH THE PLACE.

Ash Kapoor had been away too long. Although she had kept up with her friends since moving away, she hadn't seen Woodsword Middle School in a while.

There were a lot of little changes, which she noticed right away. The gardening club had been hard at work, and flowers were in bloom in little gardens all over the school grounds. The school's ancient, rusty weathervane had been replaced with a shiny new model in the shape of an atom. **(That had to be Doc's doing.)** While riding in on the bus, she had even spotted a beehive!

But the important things hadn't changed at all.

For example, her friends still gave the best group hugs.

"**Okay, enough hugging!**" said Morgan, pulling free from their group embrace. "We've got to update Ash on everything that's happened."

"Brace yourself," warned Jodi.

"So it isn't good news," said Ash. "**Has the Fault gotten worse?**"

"That's an understatement," said Theo. "The last time we played, the Overworld was ninety percent Fault."

"But that's not the worst of it," said Harper. "Our VR goggles were destroyed in the flood."

"Oh no!" said Ash. "So there's only one left?"

"No," said Morgan. "**All five were wrecked.**"

"But Doc made six of them," said Ash. "Remember?" She dug around in her backpack. "I took one with me, when I moved." **Grinning, she pulled something from the pack and held it out for them all to see.** "And I brought it with me."

Everyone's eyes went wide. They all started talking at once.

"I can't believe we forgot. . . ."

"Ash to the rescue . . . again"

". . . have a real chance now."

". . . corn dogs for lunch."

Morgan, however, was quiet. His lower lip trembled with emotion. Then he leapt forward, his arms held out wide. "One more hug, everybody!" he cried. "Come on! Everybody get in on this!"

Ash smiled. It was good to be back. **For a moment, it felt like she'd never left.**

But then there was a tremendous crash. It echoed through the gymnasium, so loud and sudden that Ash nearly dropped the headset right out of her hands.

"Careful!" said Morgan.

"I've got it," said Ash. "But what was that sound?"

"It wasn't thunder," said Harper. **"It sounded like a train hit the school."**

"Or a ravager," said Po. "Which I actually had a dream about last night." He gasped. **"Does this mean I'm psychic?!"**

"No," said Theo.

Po gasped again. "I knew you'd say that!"

Ash noticed that Doc and Ms. Minerva were hurrying out into the hallway. "We should follow them," she suggested. "If we want to see for ourselves what just happened."

Jodi led the way. She put on a pair of sunglasses,

popped up her collar, and stepped lightly on her feet. **Ash recognized Jodi's "spy mode" immediately.** But there was no need to be sneaky. Plenty of other students had wandered into the hallway, curious about the noise.

Doc and Ms. Minerva were both running ahead. **"So much for no running in the halls,"** Po said.

The teachers came to a stop before a closed classroom door. Ash wondered how they knew this was the source of the sound they'd heard.

Then she saw water seeping out from beneath the door. It pooled in the center of the hallway.

"My lab!" cried Doc.

Ms. Minerva pushed the door open just as Ash and the others caught up. Ash peered around the teacher. Her jaw dropped at what she saw.

A tree had fallen outside and crashed right through a window in Doc's laboratory classroom. **Rain poured into the opening, and sodden leaves and fragmented branches littered the tabletops.** At least one microscope lay broken on the ground.

Ash had never seen such destruction in a classroom. It was as if Woodsword was under siege. **And the storm wasn't finished yet.**

Chapter 4

ASH STANDS ALONE! SHE ALSO RUNS, JUMPS, AND FIGHTS ALONE. BUT I'M SURE SHE'S GOT THIS. SHE'S VERY CAPABLE!

The damaged lab was quickly blocked off and the hallway mopped, and **school resumed as normal, although students and teachers all watched the classroom windows with concern.** While Morgan and the others tried to focus on their school lessons, Ash and the rest of the visiting Wildling Scouts spent the day across the street at Stonesword Library.

Hours later, after a full day of carrying ruined books and furniture out to a dumpster, Ash's muscles ached. She wanted a shower and a nap.

But her friends needed her. **The Evoker King needed her.** Ash decided that going into Minecraft might actually reinvigorate her.

The decision wasn't that difficult when she saw the look of pure exhilaration on Harper's face.

They were meeting in the cafetorium, with Ms. Minerva's permission. She'd even given them some snacks: fresh fruit and little cartons of milk.

"I've got an idea," Harper said. "Mr. Mallory mentioned that the library's computers are still on, and that should include the networked PC we use for Minecraft. If I can connect your headset to that computer remotely by piggybacking off the school's Wi-Fi, **then one of us should be able to get into the game from here."**

"That all makes sense, kind of," said Ash. "But why is Po covered in aluminum foil?"

"Because I'm helping!" said Po. He held a spoon high up in the air. **"It's possible that by taking on the aspect of a giant antenna,**

I'll boost the signal and help Harper's plan work."

"It is technically possible," said Theo. He rubbed his chin doubtfully. "Likely? No. Possible? Sure."

"**Good enough for me!**" said Po, pulling out a second spoon and holding it in the air.

Harper turned back to Ash. "Doc's already

boosted the school Wi-Fi to a ridiculous extreme. That's what makes this plan possible. Well, that and your headset."

"**Which is why you should be the one to go into the game,**" said Morgan.

"Me?" said Ash. "I was sure *you* would want to."

"I do," said Morgan, smiling. "**But I've gotten better at sharing.** And it's your headset, so fair is fair." His smile dropped. "But be *careful.* It felt like the entire Overworld was falling apart. Who knows what you'll find when you connect?"

"Only one way to answer that," said Ash, and she donned her goggles. "**I'm ready when you are, Harper.**"

With Morgan's warning ringing in her ears, Ash expected the worse as she pulled the goggles into place and logged in.

To her surprise, her avatar appeared just where she'd left it, on a tranquil, grassy plain, near a smattering of flowers. The sun was just peeking over a snow-capped mountain range, and Ash's bed, chest, and inventory were all just as she remembered.

So far, so good.

A low groan alerted her to new danger. She turned to see a zombie approaching her from the edge of a heavily shaded forest. As it stepped into the sunlight, the zombie's

skin should have burst into flame.

But the zombie didn't burst into flame. It didn't seem bothered by the sun at all.

And Ash was standing there, unarmed.

"Sword," she mumbled. **"WHERE'S MY SWORD?"**

She quickly rifled through her inventory, selecting her best weapon: a diamond sword, enchanted with Sharpness. It would make exceptionally short work of a lowly zombie. Even if that zombie seemed strangely unbothered by sunlight.

Ash thrust with her sword.

But the sword never connected with the mob.

She watched in amazement as her weapon broke apart into pixels before

her very eyes. One moment it was a gleaming sword. The next it was gone. A few stray pixels floated away, as if carried off by the wind.

But there was no wind in Minecraft, of course.

Or was there? Ash suddenly had to rethink everything she thought she knew about the game. **The zombie swiped at her, growling.** Ash was strangely relieved that the zombie, at least, was acting like a zombie.

She swiped back, hitting it with her bare, blocky fist. The zombie was knocked backward—

And the block beneath it broke apart as if it had been hit with a powerful pickaxe. Grass and dirt shattered apart. The zombie fell through the new hole . . . **and kept falling.**

Ash crept carefully to the edge and peered inside. It was too dark to see very far, but she had the impression that the hole went a very long way indeed. Perhaps all the way down to bedrock.

Then she wondered: *Does bedrock even exist anymore?*

As Ash watched, the blue sky glitched out, replaced by black. The sun still hung in the sky, but it gave off little light. And the one-block-wide hole at Ash's feet began to grow larger, one block at a time.

The Overworld wasn't just broken and in

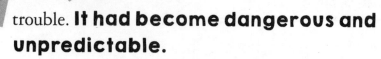

trouble. **It had become dangerous and unpredictable.**

And there was no sign of the one thing she so desperately hoped to see.

"Where are you, butterflies?" she asked. **"WHERE IS THE FINAL PIECE OF THE EVOKER KING?"**

The pixelated sky only grew darker and gave no answer.

Chapter 5

THE WISDOM OF BUTTERFLIES: EMBRACE CHANGE. SEEK SHELTER FROM THE STORM. AND EAT YOUR GREENS!

Morgan **listened anxiously as Ash spoke.** She told them all about her zombie encounter, the disappearing sword, and the bottomless pit. When the sky had glitched out, she'd quickly disconnected, and Morgan didn't blame her.

It sounded totally chaotic. And dangerous. Far too dangerous for any one of them to go in alone.

"We need more goggles," he said. "It's the only way."

"I tried," Harper said. "Mr. Mallory let me take a pair home. **All the electronics inside** were totally fried."

"So we can't fix them," said Po. "Can we make new ones?"

"We can't," said Theo. "But we know someone who might be able to."

Jodi opened the cafetorium door and peered through the rain. **"Her car's still in the parking lot. She hasn't left yet!"**

"Okay." Morgan smiled despite all the grim details Ash had shared. This was starting to sound like an actual plan. "Doc made the original goggles.

So we'll ask her to do it again." He clapped his hands together. **"Let's find her! Come on!"**

Doc wasn't in her laboratory classroom, sorting through the wreckage. She wasn't in the teachers' lounge. Just as Morgan began to worry they wouldn't find her, Po squeaked.

"I saw her through that window," he said. **"She's in the butterfly sanctuary!"**

Morgan chuckled. He'd honestly forgotten that the school had a room just for butterflies. It had once been Woodsword's computer lab, before the insects had taken over.

"Oh!" said Ash. "I've never seen it in person."

"Then you're in for a treat," said Harper.

"Unless you dislike insects," added Theo. "If you dislike insects, you really won't enjoy this at all."

Judging by the excitement on her face, Ash did not dislike insects. She opened the door, and **she motioned for the others to hurry inside, before any butterflies could escape.**

Doc was holding a terrarium in her hands.

It was like an aquarium, but full of leafy plants instead of water. Morgan counted at least four cocoons attached to those plants. He leaned in for a closer look . . . and then a butterfly landed on the tip of his nose.

"It tickles!" he said.

"It's a good look for you," Ash said in a teasing voice. "The wings really bring out the color of your eyes."

"How about the color of his cheeks?" said Jodi. "He's blushing!"

"I am not," said Morgan, and he blew the butterfly off his nose.

"Hello, Ash," said Doc. "It's good to have you back, even if it's just for a little while."

"Thanks, Doc," said Ash. **"Are you gathering cocoons?"**

"I am," said the teacher. "This used to be our computer lab. But I'm sure you remember that. You spent a lot of time here!"

"Those were the best weeks of her life," said Po, pretending to sniffle with emotion.

"Anyway, after the incident at the laboratory, we need all the space we can get," Doc explained. "I'm going to set the adult butterflies free. And I'll find a safe place where the cocooned ones can finish their metamorphosis."

"Are you injecting them with super chemicals?" asked Jodi. "Mutating the butterflies into giant beasts you can ride into battle with the school board?"

"I like the way you think," said Doc. "But Minerva made me promise not to do any genetic tampering on school grounds, alas. Care to help me gather the remaining cocoons?"

"**I'll help,**" said Harper, perking up at the chance to assist her favorite teacher.

Theo cleared his throat. "Actually, we're here to ask *you* for help, Doc."

"These VR goggles you made." Ash held up the last remaining pair. "They're very special to us. But we lost five of them when the library flooded. Do you think you could make new ones?"

"And quickly?" added Theo.

Harper shushed him. "**Theo, be polite!**"

"I'd rather be honest," said Theo. "We need more headsets in order to help the artificial—"

"*Our friend,*" Morgan interrupted. "**We need more headsets so we can help our friend.**"

"It sounds very serious indeed," said Doc. "But I don't have all the parts I would need. It could be weeks before I can rebuild even a single set." On seeing their reactions, Doc laughed. "Don't look so glum!" she said. "There's a quick, temporary solution to your problem. Look here."

Doc took Ash's headset in her hands. She lifted a small panel to reveal input and output jacks. "These goggles were meant to be networked. In fact, with a few ethernet cables, a memory card or two, and dollar-store sunglasses, **you could rig up a whole circuit of VR goggles by piggybacking off the software of this single pair.**" She handed the goggles back to Ash. "I'm sure Harper can handle it, but I'm available if you have trouble."

"**I can do that!**" said Harper excitedly. Morgan hadn't totally understood, but Harper seemed to grasp exactly what Doc was suggesting. "I've got everything we need except sunglasses."

"I've got you covered," said Jodi. She turned her backpack upside down, and several pairs of sunglasses in different styles fell out.

"Why?" asked Po. "Just . . . why?"

Jodi shrugged. "They're for my spy kit. **You can never have too many disguises.**"

"I accept this explanation," said Po, and he chose a glittery pink pair from the pile.

"There's one more thing I have to do," said Doc. "The rain has stopped for a moment, so now's my chance. Everybody ready?"

Morgan wasn't sure what he needed to be ready for. So he was caught by surprise when Doc threw open the nearest window.

Wind swirled around the room. **The adult butterflies immediately took notice,** and one by one flew out of the classroom and into the late-afternoon sky.

"Will they be okay?" asked Morgan.

"They'll be marvelous," said Doc. **"After all, they were born to fly.** And we could all learn a thing or two from butterflies."

"Like what?" asked Po.

"Embrace change," answered Doc. She was smiling as she watched all the colorful insects fly into the distance.

Chapter 6

WEARING SUNGLASSES INDOORS? TOTALLY ACCEPTABLE IF THEY'RE HOT-WIRED WITH IMPROVISED VR TECH!

Po had to admit it: he was impressed. Where yesterday there had been one set of VR glasses, now there were six. **The styles ranged from classic aviators to sci-fi new-wave shades**—all with wires and computer-chip gizmos attached.

"Harper, you're amazing! You did all this last night?" he asked.

Harper smiled at the compliment. "It was easy once Doc explained how it worked," she said. "I'm just glad Jodi had so many sets of sunglasses."

"I feel a little silly," said Theo. He was

trying on a set of goggles that clearly belonged at a swimming pool.

"**You look awesome**," Po promised. "Honestly, it's about time this group started experimenting with new styles."

"I don't care how we look," Morgan said. **His glasses were oversized and clunky,** as if they belonged in an old-school video game. "I'd wear a burlap sack and mismatched socks if it got us back into Minecraft."

"I'm with Morgan on that," said Ash. "We only have a little bit of time before you have to be in class and I have to be at the library." She slipped her goggles on. "**Let's make the most of our time.**"

Po gasped as his digital form took shape. Evidence of the Fault was all around him. He saw it in the black sky. He saw it in a strangely glitching tree, which seemed to blink in and out of existence.

But that wasn't why Po was gasping.

He was gasping . . . **because his avatar was half bee and half axolotl.**

And that was awesome.

"Look at me!" he cried. "Look at me!"

"Oh no!" said Jodi. "Your skins got all mixed up."

But Po was laughing. "I'm a whole new creature! CALL ME A BUMBLOTL!"

"I won't call him that,"
Theo said to the group.
"BE CAREFUL, PO,"
Morgan warned. "I can tell
you're excited, but we should
all stay close together."

**"MY SWORD IS BACK
IN MY INVENTORY,"** Ash
said, and she drew a diamond
blade. "But . . . I think it's
got a different enchantment
than before."

**"THERE DOESN'T SEEM TO BE ANY
RHYME OR REASON TO ANY OF THIS,"** said
Harper. She was standing in a patch of snow.

"You can say that again," said Jodi, who stood
next to Harper. Yet Jodi appeared to be in a
miniature desert biome, complete with sand and
a cactus.

**Morgan bonked his fists against his
square forehead.** "I feel like I'm losing my
mind!" he said. "Minecraft is supposed to have
rules. And I have all those rules memorized. But

this . . . ? It's just absolute chaos!"

"**WE'LL FIX IT,**" Ash promised. "We'll find the last piece of the Evoker King. Fixing him will fix the game. Right?"

Theo shrugged his blocky shoulders. "That's our theory. **AND IT'S JUST A THEORY.** But it's the best idea we've got."

"Then we need to find the butterflies," said Jodi. "They've led us to all the other pieces."

"**IT'S GOING TO BE LIKE FINDING A NEEDLE IN A HAYSTACK,**" said Po. "If the haystack was moving. And occasionally transformed into a bear."

"Well, here's some good news," said Theo, and he swung his pickaxe into the dirt. "We can still mine."

"**AND WE CAN STILL CRAFT!**" added Harper. She lifted a freshly crafted sword from a crafting table. "As long as we can do those things, we can survive here."

Jodi picked up the dirt block that Theo had knocked loose. "**LET'S BUILD A TOWER,**" she suggested. "Maybe from up high, we'll be able to see what we're looking for."

Po joined in. "I've got a lot of cobblestone. **WE CAN USE IT TO BUILD.**"

But as Po began laying the foundations for a tower, he noticed something strange. The blocks he set down were a variety of colors, each different from the last. "Do you all see this?" he asked.

"THAT'S NOT COBBLESTONE," said Theo.

"It was cobblestone when it was in my inventory!" insisted Po.

Everyone gathered around, and those with extra building materials pitched in. It was the same for everybody. They would try to place cobblestone, but the block they set seemed to be chosen at random. Sometimes Po could barely tell the difference. He couldn't always distinguish one type of stone block from another. But as blocks of obsidian, glass, slime, and dyed wool appeared, nobody could deny what was happening.

"THIS IS TOO WEIRD," said Harper.

"But sort of beautiful," said Jodi.

Po stepped back to look at their build. Jodi was right. Their watchtower was an odd mismatch of colors and materials. But it was strangely nice to look at.

And the build paid off almost immediately. From the top, Ash shouted, **"A BUTTERFLY! I SEE ONE!"**

Po whirled around. Down

on the ground, he was nearest to it. He took off in pursuit, while the others followed close behind.

They didn't make it far before they came to the edge of the plains biome. **Normally, that wouldn't have been a problem.** Normally, one Minecraft biome blended into another, and another.

But there was nothing normal about this situation. The biome ended in a sheer drop into an inky void. From the edge, Po could see a swamp biome floating nearby, and a jungle biome beyond that. A great mass of ocean floated in the distance. It didn't appear to be connected to anything. It was like a great blue bubble suspended in space.

It looked like the game was being pulled apart into separate pieces. **The Overworld was a collection of disconnected islands.**

"WE NEED TO BUILD A BRIDGE," said Morgan.

Jodi put a steadying hand on his shoulder. "It's too late. The butterfly's gone."

"And we just used up most of our building materials on the watchtower," Po said.

Morgan grimaced. "WE ALMOST HAD IT!"

"This is a good thing," said Theo. "Now we know we're close."

"AND WE HAVE A DIRECTION TO TRAVEL," added Harper.

"If we work together, we can do this!" said Ash.

"That's right," said Po. He clapped Morgan on the back. "Cobblestone let you down? Don't worry, bud." He grinned. "WE'LL BE YOUR ROCK."

Chapter 7
THE DUCHESS ON HOLIDAY! (ALSO, THERE ARE SOME IMPORTANT PLOT DEVELOPMENTS, BUT IT WILL BE A WHILE BEFORE THEIR RELEVANCE BECOMES APPARENT.)

Even after spending time in Minecraft that morning, Morgan and the others still arrived early to homeroom. Ms. Minerva sat at her desk grading papers. Nearby, a wastebasket was set out to catch water droplets from the leaky ceiling.

The storm seemed to be passing, but not quickly enough for Morgan. He didn't know how much more rain and wind the school could take!

Jodi ignored the wastebasket and ran over to the hamster cages. "I need to see how Duchess Dimples is adjusting to her vacation home!" she said.

"Vacation?" echoed Ms. Minerva. "I'm afraid it might be a permanent relocation."

Thunder rumbled outside, making the teacher's statement sound ominous.

"Permanent? What do you mean?" asked Morgan.

Ms. Minerva realized she'd spoken louder than she'd intended. "Oh! Of course Dimples is welcome to stay as long as she likes. She's not the problem. **I'm simply worried that the library will never be entirely fixed."**

"But . . . why not?" asked Po. "Ash and her troop are over there now. They're helping Mr. Mallory clean up the mess."

"That's true," said Ms. Minerva. "But the scouts can't replace the roof. And I'm afraid that the people of this town don't care enough about the library to save it."

"No way!" said Po. "The library is awesome. We used it to learn about bees."

"And code-breaking," Harper added.

"I've got a backpack full of programming books that I checked out," said Theo. "It's weighs a ton. I can barely lift it!"

Ms. Minerva smiled. "That's a pleasant surprise. I thought you were only going to the library to use the computers."

"Well, that, too," Theo confessed. "But that's what makes the library—or media center, or whatever you want to call it—so special. There are books and computers and electronic media like DVDs. There are even board games you can check out."

"And classes!" Jodi said, turning away momentarily from

the hamster cages. "Our mom attended a basket-weaving class there."

Ms. Minerva's smile deepened. "Well, good!" she said. "Perhaps I was worried for nothing. Perhaps this town *does* care about its library."

"As much as Baron Sweetcheeks cares about Duchess Dimples, I bet," said Jodi. **"look at these little fur balls!** They're having so much fun."

Morgan looked over at the cages, and he saw that they had been connected by a piece of PVC pipe. That way, each hamster had their own space, but they could also visit each other. **At the moment, Duchess Dimples was using Baron Sweetcheeks's exercise wheel** while the baron watched her. **It almost looked**

like he was cheering her on!

And Morgan remembered when Ms. Minerva had cheered them on. She had watched over them during their conflict with the Evoker King, using one of the headsets to appear in the game as a mysterious figure they knew only as the Librarian. **It was easy to forget, sometimes, that his teacher loved Minecraft, too.**

"We should tell you what's going on in our game," said Morgan. "Things have gotten . . . a little out of hand."

And to the surprise of his friends, Morgan told her everything. About how they'd befriended the Evoker King. **About how the Evoker King had split apart into six different mobs.** About the Fault that appeared in the sky at around the same time. About how that Fault had grown and seemed ready to swallow the entire game.

"That all sounds very stressful," said Ms. Minerva. **"Have you considered starting a new game?** You don't need Doc's strange technology to enjoy it. I've been logging a lot of hours at home. I've just built my forty-third bookshelf!"

Morgan shook his head. "We can't just leave our game behind. **Not until we know if the Evoker King can be saved.**"

"I respect that," said Ms. Minerva as their other classmates began filing in for homeroom. "And I'm glad you told me about it. Doesn't it feel good to share?"

"It does," Morgan confessed. And it was true. **He felt a little less worried** now that he'd spoken his worries out loud.

"There's a lesson in there somewhere," said

Ms. Minerva. "Secrets and exclusive clubs are fun. But they can make us feel all alone with our problems. **The bigger your community, the smaller your problems can become.**"

"We'll keep it in mind," said Morgan. But he was eager to change the subject. His classmates were listening in now, and they seemed curious to know what Ms. Minerva was talking about. And despite Ms. Minerva's advice, **Morgan wasn't ready for everyone to know his business.**

Chapter 8

IT'S TOTALLY VEXING, BUT LET'S GO OVER A FEW THINGS FOR THOSE WHO HAVEN'T BEEN PAYING ATTENTION. WE'RE LOOKING AT YOU, PO.

After school, they gathered once again in Minecraft. Jodi was on high alert for anything strange. **"LET'S NOT WASTE BUILDING MATERIALS THIS TIME,** if we can avoid it," she suggested.

Before Doc had invented the VR goggles, Jodi had played Creative Mode. She still missed flying sometimes. Flying would have come in handy when they were hunting the strange Minecraft butterflies!

"I WANT TO TRY SOMETHING," she said. "A sort of art project."

"I'm not sure now's the time," said Theo.

"It'll only take a minute," Jodi said. "Do you still have one of the Evoker King's legs? **GIVE IT HERE!**"

Her time in Survival Mode had taught Jodi a lot about combat and resource management. But what she would always love most about Minecraft was that it allowed her to make art.

The others had set down their Evoker King pieces. **Jodi began putting the pieces together like a jigsaw puzzle.** She started with the legs.

"I see what she's doing," said Harper. "Do you think this will work, Theo?"

Theo shrugged. **"IT'S WORTH A TRY,"** he said. "But without the final piece, there's still a hole in the code."

"Explain that to me," said Ash. "I've never fully understood the connection between the Evoker King and the Fault."

"OH, GOOD! I THOUGHT IT WAS JUST ME," said Po. "Sometimes I zone out a little bit. Especially when Theo and Harper talk about coding and math."

As Theo watched Jodi connect the Evoker King's torso, he said, "The Evoker King was never supposed to be a part of the game. He was an invasive artificial intelligence who accessed the game through Doc's high-tech virtual reality equipment."

"Like an invasive species," Harper suggested. "IN THE REAL WORLD, SOMETIMES ANIMALS THAT DON'T BELONG IN A PARTICULAR ECOSYSTEM FIND THEIR WAY INTO THAT ECOSYSTEM. Because they have different ways of surviving than the normal species in that environment, everything can get thrown out of balance."

". . . so science stuff?" Po said.

"Right," said Theo. "But in this case, the game and the invader found a new balance. The Evoker King, who is made up of programming code, and this game of Minecraft, which is also made up of programming code, grew intertwined. When the Evoker King transformed, he left a hole right in the heart of the game's code. And the hole has been expanding. It's like a sweater slowly unstitching because somebody pulled on a thread."

"But a sweater can be knit back together . . . ," Ash said.

"Exactly," said Theo. "And we hope the code

will fix itself once the Evoker King is put back together and the hole gets plugged."

Jodi had finished assembling the various Evoker King fragments. There was a torso, two arms, and two legs. But they were still missing one crucial piece.

"He looks like a Christmas tree without a star on top," said Ash.

"OR A HEADLESS SCARECROW," said Morgan.

"Ooh! That gives me an idea," said Po. He approached the headless form and plopped a carved pumpkin on top.

They all waited expectantly.

"I guess that didn't do anything," said Harper.

"Sure it did," said Po. "It made me feel better."

Jodi cocked her head to give the pumpkin-headed creation a good look. It was obvious to her that they needed to find the Evoker King's true head. She stepped forward to remove the pumpkin.

And she saw something blue out of the corner of her eye.

She thought it was a butterfly. She turned around quickly, already pointing.

To her surprise, it wasn't a butterfly at all. It was blue, but a much paler shade than the butterflies she'd seen. Like a butterfly, it flew, but on tattered, wispy wings. **It was small, shaped like a human, and held a dark sword in one of its hands.**

So: definitely not a butterfly.

"IT'S A VEX!" said her brother.

"But . . . that doesn't make sense," said Theo. "What would a vex be doing out here?"

Seeing the confusion on Jodi's face, Ash explained, **"NORMALLY, A VEX ONLY APPEARS WHEN SUMMONED BY AN EVOKER."**

Everyone's eyes went wide at the same time.

They looked from the partially completed Evoker King to the vex, and they knew: **this was the final mob they needed.**

"Grab it!" cried Morgan, and he lunged forward.

The vex easily dodged him, flying just beyond his reach.

Jodi dashed forward. The vex was now flying

in her direction. "I'll box it in," she said, and she began laying blocks in a wall formation.

To her surprise, the wall didn't stop the vex. It passed right through the blocks, like a ghost.

"Hey, that isn't fair," complained Jodi.

Po waved a sword at the vex as it approached him.

"DON'T HURT IT," warned Harper.

"I'm not!" said Po. "I'm trying to get it to fly in the other direction."

"Oh, good idea, Po," said Ash. "If we can get it to land on the Evoker King's empty shoulders, then all his pieces will be in the right place!"

"TALK TO IT!" said Theo. "That worked with the other Evoker Spawn."

"Mr. Vex," said Po. "Please stop being so vexing!"

"It's not going to listen," Jodi said. She could see in the mob's erratic flight pattern that it was upset. **"WE'VE SCARED IT, AND NOW IT JUST WANTS TO GET AWAY."**

"Please don't go!" said Morgan, but as they

watched, the vex passed through the ground.

Morgan ran forward, lifting his pickaxe high. He began digging frantically near the spot where the vex had disappeared.

But it didn't do any good. **The mob was nowhere to be found.**

Chapter 9

I SCREAM! YOU SCREAM! THEN WE GET IN TROUBLE FOR YELLING, SO WE USE OUR INSIDE VOICES TO ASK POLITELY FOR ICE CREAM.

Dark clouds blanketed the sky, and thunder rumbled in the distance. **But the rain, at last, had stopped falling, and the wind had calmed to a gentle breeze.** Ash was happy for the break in the weather. She was only in town for a few more days, after all, and she still had several favorite locations she wanted to visit.

There was the bat house that she had helped build, on the edge of school property. A bookstore that had a huge selection of graphic novels and manga. **And the best ice cream shop around, with dozens of flavors and uncountable toppings.**

She asked Morgan to join her for ice cream. She thought it was about time the two of them had a very important talk. **And she was worried that he wouldn't like what she had to say.**

But in Ash's experience, ice cream made everything a little bit better.

That was especially true about ice cream with a friend. And not just human friends. Morgan had gotten permission to bring the hamsters home for the evening. **Baron Sweetcheeks and Duchess Dimples were each in their own plastic ball,** rolling around at Ash's feet.

"It's so hard to choose," Ash said as they waited

in line. **"There are so many options!"**

"Yeah," Morgan agreed. But when it was his turn to order at the shop window, he asked for a cup of simple vanilla ice cream.

They sat on a nearby swing set, and Morgan's eyes bounced between his plain white scoop and the multicolored confection Ash had chosen: **three flavors of ice cream, topped with bright sprinkles, gummies, walnuts, and a drizzle of butterscotch.**

Ash laughed as Morgan goggled. "You can't get this specific combination anywhere near my house," she explained.

"It looks so chaotic," he said. "Is it *good*?"

"Of course it's good," Ash answered, and she licked her lips. "It's all sugar, after all."

"I guess I could be a bit more daring," Morgan said. "But I get worried about what could happen. I know for a fact that I like vanilla ice cream. **So why risk getting something I won't like as much?"**

Ash laughed again. "Because you might find something you like even more. **You can't know unless you try!"**

"I guess," Morgan replied, looking skeptical.

Ash watched him poke at his ice cream with his spoon. She took a breath. It was now or never.

"That's actually what I wanted to talk to you about," said Ash.

Morgan looked confused. "My ice cream selection?"

"No," said Ash. **"Your reluctance to try new things."**

"Oh." Morgan watched the hamsters rolling around beneath his feet. "This sounds serious."

"It's not a big deal," Ash promised. "It's just that I have an idea. **And I want to make sure you really listen to it.** And I hope that you'll consider it before you try to shoot it down."

"I don't shoot ideas down," Morgan said a little defensively. Then he added, "Do I?"

"Not always," said Ash. "But when we

needed help deciphering a code, I thought we should ask my Wildling troop for help. **And you weren't happy about that.**"

"Well, that's certainly true . . . ," said Morgan. He took a scoop of ice cream without taking a bite.

"Or what about our decision to let Theo join the club? You didn't like that." She grinned. "And you were the same way when I joined, remember?"

"That was a long time ago!" Morgan said, leaning back in his swing. **"I've changed.** I'm way more relaxed and open."

"Good," said Ash. "In that case, I've got an idea." She pulled a sheet of graphing paper from her pocket with her free hand before unfolding it and handing it to Morgan. **The paper contained her design for something she was calling a slime engine.** "Really, it was Po's idea. He inspired me when he tried to force the vex to move toward the Evoker King fragments. This device should help us do that."

Morgan took a moment to wrap his head around Ash's design. She had labeled everything clearly, but there were a lot of different elements. **The slime engine made use of sticky pistons, redstone blocks, and slime blocks.** But at heart, the idea was simple. The slime engine would crawl forward on its own, using a wall of slime to push anything in its path.

"Because slime blocks can push vexes!" Morgan said. He wanted to slap his forehead with the realization, but his hands were full of ice cream and blueprints. "Ash, this is brilliant." He furrowed his brow. "Only, to cover a large space, we'd need a lot of these engines, all coming from different directions."

"Right. My thinking exactly," said Ash. "And that brings us to the part I'm nervous to say out loud, but here goes: Morgan, I think we should invite more kids to join us in Minecraft."

"No way!" Morgan said automatically. "Our team is special. And it's hard enough getting Po and Jodi to take it seriously sometimes. And the Evoker King is depending on us, and, and—

I'm doing the thing where I shoot down an idea, aren't I?"

Ash took a prim bite of her ice cream and gave him an innocent shrug that said *What do you think?*

Morgan sighed loudly. **"I'm sorry. I'll hear you out."**

"Thank you," said Ash. She anchored her feet and twisted her swing around so that she was facing him. "Here's the thing. Keeping our club or whatever you want to call it secret made sense when we only had a few headsets. **But if we can make five of them, we can make ten. Maybe more!** And with that many of us working together, we can build these slime engines, find the vex, and restore the Evoker King. At least, we'll have a better chance of doing all that before time runs out."

Morgan stared into his ice cream as if it held the secrets of the universe.

"Well?" Ash said finally. "Say something."

Morgan frowned. "What if we do this . . . and nothing is ever the same again?"

"That's what change is. You can fight it or you

can embrace it. But it comes eventually, either way." Ash lifted her feet, and her swing spun around as its chains untwisted. "And wouldn't you rather embrace it, if it gives us a better chance to help the Evoker King?"

Morgan's eyes glittered in the shop's neon lights. He reached down and gently picked up Baron Sweetcheeks's hamster ball. **"What do you think, Baron?"**

Baron Sweetcheeks scratched his chin vigorously and then ran around in a small circle three times.

"You're right. We're just going to keep running in circles if we keep doing things my way," Morgan said. "And you're right, too, Ash. **To save the Evoker King ... we have to try something new."**

He stood up, sliding out of the swing.

"Where are you going?" Ash asked, surprised at his intensity. "We can't really do anything until tomorrow."

"You're wrong. There's something I can do right now," said Morgan. **"I can ask them to put sprinkles on my ice cream!"**

Ash gasped. "Are you sure?"

"I'm tired of being afraid to try new things," he said. "And to be honest, they look delicious."

"They are!" Ash said, and as the sun broke through the clouds for the first time in days, she put a spoonful of dessert into her mouth. **Nothing had ever tasted sweeter.**

Chapter 10

A BRIGHT AND SUNNY AFTERNOON! A HOPEFUL SIGN OF THINGS TO COME! NOTHING TO GO WRONG JUST YET.

The sun was finally shining outside Woodsword Middle School, but Morgan barely noticed.

Because a light of a different kind was shining inside Morgan's heart.

The bell rang, and Morgan leapt out of his chair. He was the first one out the door, and Jodi was waiting for him just outside. Her hands were stained with multicolored paints.

"I got all the posters finished and hung up," she said. "Things got a little messy."

Morgan gave her a high five. He didn't mind getting a little color on him.

The siblings hurried down the hallway. They passed the classroom where student government meetings were held. Po was there, taping a red sign to the door. It read MEETING CANCELED.

"Dude!" Po said to Morgan. He wheeled alongside Morgan and Jodi as they continued down the hallway. **"Shelly canceled today's meeting. I think she saw one of Jodi's posters."** He turned to Jodi. "Which are beautiful and excellent," he added.

Jodi beamed. "Aw, shucks. I bet you say that to everybody who uses elements of French Expressionism in their school flyers."

Po shrugged. "I like color."

They ran into Harper and Theo soon after.

"Today's the day," said Theo. "Are you sure this is a good idea?"

"I just hope I made enough headsets," said Harper.

"We're about to find out," said Morgan. He pushed open the doors to the cafetorium.

Just as he'd hoped, **a group of eager students was waiting on the other side.**

"Are we in the right place?" asked Shelly Silver. She held up one of Jodi's flyers, still wet with paint. **"Is this the Minecraft club?"**

Morgan realized that she had directed the question at him. Everyone's eyes looked his way, and he felt queasy. He tried not to let them see how nervous he was. He forced himself to grin. He hoped it looked like the confident smile of a leader.

"You're in the right place," he said. "Thanks for coming, everybody."

Morgan looked over the crowd. There were about a dozen kids there, and he recognized all of them. He saw several of Po's basketball teammates, a couple of drama kids, some cheerleaders, and more. Ash waved at a few Wildling Scouts. Even Po's older cousin Hope was there.

"I'm here as the chaperone," Hope explained, and **she handed Morgan a small corn dog on a stick.** "And to promote my new food truck."

Ned Brant, a reporter for the school's podcast, held a microphone in Morgan's direction. "Can you tell us why the Blockheadz are so eager for new members?"

"We're not calling ourselves that," Morgan grumbled.

Theo crossed his arms, bashfully hiding the BLOCKHEADZ logo on his T-shirt.

"We asked you here to help us with an experiment," Harper explained, and she began passing out the jury-rigged sunglasses. "We've got some pretty fun technology built into these glasses. It's a whole new way to play Minecraft!"

"But there's bad news, too," said Morgan. "The Minecraft you're about to experience is broken. We need your help to accomplish a specific task. If you get into trouble, don't worry. Hope will be able to unplug your glasses, and you'll be safely back here."

"Back here?" echoed Shelly. "I don't understand. Where are we going?"

Morgan grinned. **"Into the game."**

Chapter 11

TWO IS COMPANY. THREE IS A CROWD. BUT WITH ODDS LIKE THESE? THE MORE THE MERRIER!

Ash had never seen Minecraft so crowded.

And it had never been so loud, either.

"WOO-HOO!" cried Ned as he punched a tree into free-floating blocks of wood.

"This is so cool!" Shelly shouted. She ran her hands over a sheep. "It feels so real."

"*A-W-E-S-O-M-E!*" Tony the cheerleader spelled out.

"Po, is that you?" asked Raul, one of Po's basketball teammates. "Why do you look like a cat?"

"Maybe the question is why don't *you* look like a cat?" asked Po, who was wearing a cat suit.

Raul seemed to think this was very deep. "Huh," he said, nodding slowly.

"BUT WHAT'S WRONG WITH THE SKY?" asked Ricky, another teammate of Po's. "And why aren't the biomes connected? It all seems . . . disconnected." Ricky tapped the headless Evoker King, but nothing happened.

"Inquiring minds want to know," said Ned.

"Why is there a phantom out during the daytime?"

"PHANTOM?" echoed Harper. "Where?"

But the answer was soon obvious. The flying undead mob swept down from the sky, cutting a path through the players. Shelly was nearly knocked off her feet. Raul took a swing with a brand-new wooden sword, but the phantom had already flown beyond his reach.

"It's circling back around," said Ned.

"Raul, Raul, you can do it," cheered Tony.

"Come on now, there's nothing to it!" added Po.

The phantom flew low again, aiming for Raul, who readied his sword.

"Wait, be careful," Ash warned. "We don't know if—"

Before Ash could finish her sentence, the

phantom began to flash red. It reminded Ash of how a creeper flashed . . . right before exploding.

"RAUL, GET CLEAR!" she cried.

Raul barely jumped out of the way in time. The phantom exploded, taking a big chunk of the plains biome with it. Now there was a gaping hole at the base of their mismatched watchtower. Ash hurried over to plug it up and to check on Raul.

"I'm okay," he said. "But why did that thing explode? AND WHY WAS IT OUT IN THE DAYLIGHT TO BEGIN WITH?"

"That's what I meant when I said this version of the game is breaking down," said Morgan. "The code has gotten all wrong. We're never sure what's going to happen next."

"Which means we need to make the slime engines immediately," said Ash. "Before things get worse."

"SLIME ENGINES? What are those?" asked Shelly.

"It's what we're here to build," answered Morgan. "Ash, Po, Jodi, Harper, and I all have the design memorized. But we need materials:

redstone, wood planks, and slime. A lot of slime! Can you all help with that?"

"It's going to mean doing our best to hold this place together a little bit longer," said Harper. **"WE'LL NEED BRIDGES OR STAIRCASES TO CONNECT THE BIOMES.** We'll need to plug holes in the ground and fight off mobs that might be extra dangerous and unpredictable."

Po eyed the nearby sheep with suspicion. "Don't try anything funny," he warned them.

"THEY WOULD NEVER!" Jodi insisted.

"Tony, as a cheerleader, you're good at being heard from a distance," said Ash. "Can you climb the watchtower? **IF YOU SEE A VEX, LET US KNOW IMMEDIATELY."**

"Aye aye, captain," said Tony.

"Wildling Scouts, you're on slime ball duty."

"Where will we find slime balls?" asked a scout.

"THERE'S A SWAMP NEARBY," Morgan explained. "Make yourselves some weapons and go hunting for slimes."

Jodi added, "Or if you're not interested in combat, find some pandas! If you're lucky, a sneezing baby panda will leave a slime ball behind."

"WE'VE GOT THIS," said Shelly.

"Go team!" said Tony.

As Ash watched them, she saw the kids take

naturally to teamwork. **Ned mined,** providing the material Shelly needed to build a piston from scratch. The drama kids crafted an entire bridge, linking the plains biome to a swamp in a matter of minutes, and Wildling Scouts rushed across on their hunt for slimes.

"This could work," Morgan said beside Ash.

"I just hope we're ready before the vex appears," said Ash. "We need to be ready to seize our chance."

Morgan agreed. "Yeah," he said. **"BECAUSE IT MIGHT BE THE LAST CHANCE WE GET."**

Chapter 12

MEANWHILE: THEO'S SIDE QUEST! WHAT CHALLENGES AWAIT HIM? WILL HE REAP AN EPIC REWARD OR FACE HIS FINAL DOOM?

Theo hadn't entered the game with the rest of them. He planned to join them soon. **First he had to make sure their hardware could handle the strain.**

"And that's how you get the perfect golden-brown color," Hope was saying. **"There's nothing less appetizing than a yellow corn dog."**

"**I believe you,**" said Theo. He was only half listening. He and Harper had set up a fairly complicated computer network in the cafetorium. At the heart of the network was a single PC that Theo had brought in from home. **He had built the computer himself!** (Well, his dad had helped.) But he hadn't realized it would be pushed so hard so soon.

More than a dozen VR goggles were all using the software installed in Ash's set, which were plugged into Theo's PC, which was remotely networked to the server in the library. It was a web of connections. **And like a web, it was beautiful but delicate.** One broken thread could cause the entire thing to collapse. They just hadn't had time to make it better.

Theo was relieved to see that everything seemed to be working. It wouldn't work for long, but it didn't have to. **Just long enough for them to find that vex, herd it in the right direction, and restore the Evoker King.**

Hope finally stopped talking about corn dogs—a very strange food, in Theo's opinion. In the sudden silence, he overheard new voices. Theo realized they were coming from a little side office connected to the cafetorium. **The adult voices were hushed and urgent, and curiosity got the best of him.**

He crept closer, recognizing Ms. Minerva's voice. "I'm telling you, it's an inspiration. They're all in the game right now, working together. The rules changed on them, and they adapted."

"They're wonderful kids." That was Doc's voice. "Although the technology they're using is also pretty wonderful."

"When it works!" said Ms. Minerva.

"So we know they can adapt," said Mr. Mallory. **"That will be important if we select them for this program."**

"It sounds like we're in agreement," said Ms. Minerva. **"It will be a big change...."**

"But change can be a good thing," said Doc. "I have the paperwork right here. We can make it official."

Theo heard the rustling of papers. He peeked around the corner. All three adults were huddled over stacks of paper and manila file folders. He saw his school photo clipped to one of the folders. **Was that his permanent file?**

"This school won't be the same without them," said Ms. Minerva.

"Or without us," said Doc.

"But it's the best solution for everyone," said Mr. Mallory. "Now how about we take a break? **I was promised snacks.**"

"Po's cousin has her food truck parked outside," said Doc. "I'll treat."

"Oh, good," said Ms. Minerva. **"Who doesn't love a corn dog?"**

Chapter 13

VEXES ARE VEXING! NO SURPRISE THERE. BUT THIS ONE IS SOMETHING SPECIAL. . . .

Morgan felt a rush of relief when he saw Theo's avatar appear beside him.

"IS EVERYTHING LOOKING GOOD IRL?" he asked.

"I'm not sure," said Theo. "The adults are up to something."

"I MEAN WITH YOUR COMPUTER," said Morgan. "Everything else can wait. As long as the network is working."

"It is, for now," said Theo. "But my PC could break down at any second. **THIS MIGHT BE OUR LAST CHANCE."**

"Then we'll make the most of it," said Harper.

"JODI IS IN POSITION," said Morgan.

"And we've already built a bunch of slime engines," said Ash. "The scouts did a great job of finding slime balls."

"THERE REALLY SHOULD BE A MERIT BADGE FOR THAT," said Po.

At that moment, they heard Tony cry out, "Vex! There's a vex on the move, north by northeast!"

"IT'S TIME," said Morgan. "Come on, team. This is it!"

They hurried to the northeast edge of the plains biome. **There was a new bridge there, built by their classmates.** Its colorfully mismatched blocks made it look a little like the rainbow bridge from Norse mythology.

The bridge led to a mushroom field. Morgan saw the vex floating low among the mushrooms. **He couldn't believe their luck!** Mushroom fields were mostly flat, so the vex didn't have many places to hide.

"I'll get it over the bridge," said Morgan. "Then it will be up to the rest of you."

"I'll make sure everyone is ready," promised

Ash. "Good luck, Morgan!"

Morgan ran across the rainbow bridge, but he slowed down as he entered the first patch of mushrooms. **He didn't want to spook the vex.** It might attack him, or worse, fly away. But he had to slip past it so that he could move it in the right direction.

He constructed one more slime engine. By now, he could do it quickly. He attached a few slime blocks to a sticky piston, added some cobblestones for stability, then placed redstone blocks where they would keep the piston powered. With the push of a button, **the piston surged forward**—and because it was a sticky piston, it pulled the whole build forward.

The engine lurched ahead, a fully automated battering ram. Although something about its movement and green-and-red coloring made Morgan think of a caterpillar. An attack caterpillar! Po would get a kick out of that image.

Morgan had positioned the engine perfectly. It crept up on the vex, and when it reached the mob, the pistons slammed the slime blocks into the unsuspecting mob. **The vex was shoved forward,** onto the rainbow bridge. And as the slime engine moved forward, it continued shoving the vex all the way across the bridge and onto the plains island.

So far, so good. But would the others do their part?

"THE VEX IS BELOW!" cried Tony. "Heading southeast!"

The vex, tired of being bumped, had flown ahead of Morgan's engine. It flew past the tower, past the Evoker

King fragments, and toward the edge of the plains biome. **If it flew off into the void, it would be lost to them.**

But Shelly Silver was on the southeast edge of the island. At Tony's warning, she set her slime engine in motion. It knocked the vex back, away from the edge and toward the center of the biome.

And so it went. Po's engine in the west, Harper's engine in the northwest and Raul's to the northeast, and more. Each of them was activated in turn so that blocks of slime lurched across the biome, **closing in on the vex like a cage,** preventing it from flying off.

But it could still fly *up.*

"THE VEX IS TAKING TO THE SKIES," Ash warned.

"We'll see about that," came a voice from atop the tower. It wasn't Tony this time, but Jodi. **She leapt off the tower and into the sky!**

For a terrifying instant, Morgan watched his sister fall. But she spread the elytra that she'd kept after winning the challenge of the golem. **She drifted down,** aiming right for the vex.

Tony cheered her on from above. "Be aggressive, Jodi! *B-E* aggressive!"

"I LOVE FLYING!" she cried, and she batted

the vex downward, doing only light damage. Her aim was perfect; the vex landed atop the shoulders of the incomplete Evoker King.

Morgan held his breath. **This was it!**

As Jodi alighted on the ground, the vex still crouched atop the Evoker King's headless avatar with gleaming eyes. **It flapped its wings and made a strange giggling sound.** It appeared ready to fly away again.

"WE NEED TO TALK TO IT," said Theo. "That might calm it down."

"What should we talk about?" asked Po.

"Because I don't think I have much in common with a vex."

"Maybe not," said Ash. "On the other hand, this place—Minecraft—is the vex's home. **AND MINECRAFT HAS BEEN LIKE A SECOND HOME FOR ALL OF US.**"

"Yeah!" said Po. "It's a great place you've got here, Vexter. **WHEN I'M PLAYING MINECRAFT, I FORGET ALL MY REAL-LIFE WORRIES.** And I can stop putting so much pressure on myself to succeed. Here, I get to be whoever I want to be. **LOOK HOWEVER I WANT TO LOOK.**" Po grinned. "When I'm playing Minecraft, I feel totally free."

"I spend so much of my time worried," said Harper. "I worry about big stuff like climate change and small stuff like my grades. But in Minecraft, I don't worry so much. **HERE, EVERY PROBLEM HAS A SOLUTION.** Usually a lot of solutions, if you apply a bit of creativity!"

"It's the creativity I love most," said Jodi. "The Overworld is beautiful on its own. But it's also a canvas. **IT'S A BLANK SHEET OF PAPER**

WHERE I CAN CREATE ANYTHING I CAN DREAM UP!"

"And then you can share your creations with friends," said Ash. "I think that's my favorite part. MINECRAFT IS SOCIAL. IT BRINGS PEOPLE TOGETHER." She swept her arms out toward her friends. "It brought all of you into my life. And it kept us together when I moved away."

"I'm also grateful for the friendships," said Theo. "I CAN HAVE TROUBLE MAKING FRIENDS. LIFE IS SCARY AND CONFUSING. BUT EVERYTHING MAKES SENSE HERE. There are rules. Logic." He frowned up at the black sky. "Usually."

Suddenly, they were all looking at Morgan. "What about you?" asked Jodi.

"Yeah," said Ash. "WHAT DO YOU LOVE ABOUT MINECRAFT?"

"Everything." Morgan knew that avatars didn't cry. But he could almost swear his vision was blurring with tears. "Minecraft is all the things you said. It's art and it's science. It feels like it's my space, where I can do anything I want. But it's also something we all share." He reached out to hold hands with Ash and Po, who were closest to him. Following his lead, the others joined hands to form a circle. "Learning to share was a difficult lesson for me. BUT MY LIFE IS SO MUCH BETTER BECAUSE I'VE BEEN ABLE TO SHARE THIS ADVENTURE WITH ALL OF YOU."

While they had spoken, their schoolmates had

quietly gathered around them, and **the vex had stopped trying to escape.** It had fixed its eyes on them as they spoke, each in turn. Now, with Morgan's speech ended, the mob giggled. It began to glow.

"What did you guys do?" asked Ned.

"We're . . . not *really* certain," said Theo.

"IS THE GLOWING GOOD OR BAD?" asked Po warily.

"Let's hope for the best," said Ash.

Morgan watched intently as the vex's glow spread to the Evoker King's body, radiating down into the torso before spreading to the arms and legs. And they heard a voice:

"THANK YOU, MY FRIENDS," the familiar voice of the Evoker King boomed all around them. "Before, I transformed because of my fear and uncertainty. I needed more data to understand this world and my place in it. But now, I am whole again. And I will be in control of my next metamorphosis."

"YOU'RE CHANGING AGAIN?" asked Ash. **"WHY?"**

"I wish to experience Minecraft from . . . a new perspective."

"Wh-what do you mean?" asked Morgan.

But there was no answer.

Only a great flash of light that shone from the Evoker King . . . and grew to consume the entire Overworld.

Chapter 14

A HINT OF THINGS TO COME! BECAUSE IN MINECRAFT, WE NEVER STOP BUILDING.

Ash blinked furiously. The light had blinded her, but only for a moment. As her vision returned to her, she realized she was no longer in Minecraft. **She was back in the Woodsword cafetorium,** surrounded by students and scouts, all of them removing their headsets and rubbing their eyes.

"Oh," said Ash, and she realized her own headset was blinking red. She didn't know much about electronics, but blinking red lights were usually not good.

And Theo's computer was smoking and shooting out sparks.

"I'm on it, kids!" said Hope. **"Nobody panic!"**
As Ash watched, Po's cousin doused the computer
with a fire extinguisher. That took care of the fire
hazard. But Ash figured the computer was ruined
for good.

Theo didn't seem worried. "Did we do it?" he
asked. **"Did we succeed?"**

"I don't know what just happened," said Shelly.

"But it was awesome."

"Right?" said Po. **"Nice job, prez!"**

Morgan turned to Harper. "Why did we get booted from the game?" he asked.

Harper held a magnifying glass to the circuit board she'd welded to her sunglasses. "The whole network was overloaded. It burned out." **She put the glasses back on her face.** "These are nothing more than shades now."

"I think my headset is broken, too," said Ash. "That might have been our last hurrah."

"But did we fix the game in time?" Jodi asked. "Did we save the Evoker King? **Did we fix Minecraft?"**

"**It looked like it,**" said Theo. "But we can't know for sure until we get access to the library's computer."

"That might take a few days," said Ash. "We still have a lot of work to do at the library."

"Then we'll have to wait," said Morgan. **He watched as the kids around them all discussed their adventure excitedly.**

They didn't seem to mind that it had been cut short. **"And we just have to trust that we did everything we could,"** he added.

The very next morning, Morgan was right back in the cafetorium. The school staff had pulled

out the bleacher seats, and several teachers and administrators were on the stage. Mr. Mallory was there, too.

"Does this have something to do with the library?" Morgan asked his friends.

Theo shrugged. Po yawned. And Harper said, "*Shhh!* The assembly is starting."

Ms. Minerva welcomed them all, **and she reminded everyone about the flood at the library and the smashed school lab.** (As if anyone could forget.)

Morgan's mind began to wander. And then he thought he heard his teacher say "iron sword."

"**What was that?**" he said, a little too loudly. Jodi chuckled.

Ms. Minerva clucked her tongue. "As I was saying, the storm system has passed. But the damage done to the school and library was more extensive than we hoped. **It will take some time to make repairs, and we have no choice but to close an entire wing of the school.**"

"School's canceled?!" asked Po.

Ms. Minerva crossed her arms. "**Absolutely not.**"

Doc leaned over and took the microphone from Ms. Minerva. "What my verbose colleague is trying to say is this: To avoid overcrowding our classrooms, some Woodsword students will be attending another local school for the rest of the

school year. And they'll be joined by a few familiar teachers."

"And media specialists," added Mr. Mallory.

Morgan felt his stomach sink. He looked around at his friends. "How will you choose?" he asked. "Who stays . . . and who goes?"

"Not to worry, Morgan," said Doc. "We've taken care not to split up any tightly knit groups of friends."

"That's right," said Ms. Minerva, and she looked from Morgan to Jodi, from Po to Harper and Theo. **"Get ready for a new adventure, Minecrafters. We'll see you at the Ironsword Academy!"**

Chapter 15

EVERY ENDING IS A NEW BEGINNING. THANKS FOR ALL THE BLOCKS!

After relying on Doc's experimental VR tech for so long, Morgan felt relieved to load into their game of Minecraft the good old-fashioned way. He was using his own game controller, which was decorated with Minecraft stickers; it felt so comfortable and familiar in his hands that he almost believed it had been custom built just for him. He wore headphones to immerse himself in the sounds of the game . . . and to make it easy to chat with his friends.

For a moment, he worried that the game would be gone. What if the Fault had

spread over the Internet like a virus? What if every instance of Minecraft across the world had been consumed or warped by the crack in the code?

But his worries lifted as soon as the game loaded. **Here was Minecraft, just as he remembered it.** The Overworld had reset. The sun was high in a blue sky. The ground was solid beneath his feet.

And his friends were there at his side. Even Ash, who was back home now but able to connect from afar.

"This is what I expected, from looking at the code," said Theo. "We plugged the hole in the game's programming when we put the Evoker King back together, but it caused a full reset. **OUR ENTIRE GAME HAS BEEN REBOOTED."**

"Aw, but all our stuff!" said Po. "Our diamond pants! Our enchanted fishing rods! **MY HUGE LIBRARY OF SKINS!"**

"Sorry, Po," said Jodi, and she patted his head gently. "But look at it as an opportunity. Out with the old and in with the new."

Po perked up. "Hey! You're an artist," he said. "You want to help me design some new looks? That half bee and half axolotl skin gave me some ideas."

"I would be delighted," said Jodi, bowing.

"I'm going to ask what everyone's thinking," said Ash. **"IS THE EVOKER KING HERE SOMEWHERE?** Does he even exist anymore?"

"He said he wanted to experience the game in a new way," said Theo. "He must be here somewhere."

"Sounds like we have our first mission," said Harper. **"BUT WHERE DO WE START?"**

"We start like we always do," said Morgan. **He**

struck a tree until it produced wood.

"We gather resources. And we make tools."

"AND PETS!" said Jodi. **"WE'RE GOING TO NEED PETS!"**

"Somebody grab that pig!" said Po, and he and Jodi chased a poor confused pig in circles.

Morgan felt totally at peace. As he crafted planks and sticks from blocks of wood, he took a moment to appreciate the pleasure of starting a game from the beginning. **Everything felt so**

simple all of a sudden.

"DON'T FREAK OUT," whispered Harper. "But someone's watching us from the trees."

Po and Jodi settled down, and Morgan looked up from his work. Harper was right. A figure

stepped forward from behind a tree trunk.

Morgan braced himself for a fight. But the figure wasn't any kind of mob, hostile or otherwise. **It was a kid.**

"Hi," said the boy. "I really thought I was all alone here."

"Who are you?" asked Morgan. "Are you a Woodsword student? **DO YOU GO TO IRONSWORD?"**

"I'm not sure," said the boy. "I don't think so. **I'M . . . NEW."**

"New in what way?" asked Ash.

The boy shrugged. "Just . . . new."

"DOES HE LOOK FAMILIAR?" asked Theo.

"Yes," said Harper. "He definitely *evokes* a memory of someone we used to know."

Morgan smiled. "Let me guess. **YOU WANT TO EXPERIENCE EVERYTHING THIS WORLD HAS TO OFFER.**"

"That's right," said the boy, returning Morgan's smile. "But monsters come out at night. I could use some allies. Maybe . . . maybe some friends."

He took a hesitant step forward. "I don't know why. But I feel like I can trust you all."

"You *can* trust us," promised Ash.

"That's right," said Morgan. "You want to learn all about Minecraft? Well . . ." Morgan extended his blocky fist in greeting. **"WE'VE GOT A LOT TO SHOW YOU."**

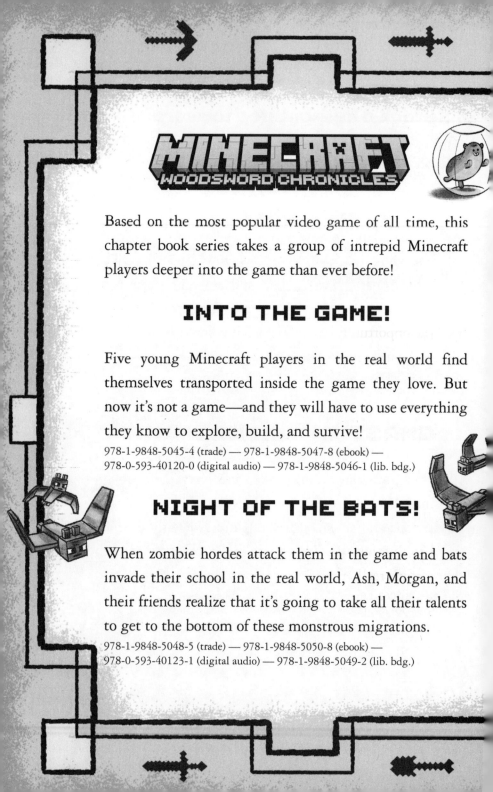

MINECRAFT
WOODSWORD CHRONICLES

Based on the most popular video game of all time, this chapter book series takes a group of intrepid Minecraft players deeper into the game than ever before!

INTO THE GAME!

Five young Minecraft players in the real world find themselves transported inside the game they love. But now it's not a game—and they will have to use everything they know to explore, build, and survive!

978-1-9848-5045-4 (trade) — 978-1-9848-5047-8 (ebook) — 978-0-593-40120-0 (digital audio) — 978-1-9848-5046-1 (lib. bdg.)

NIGHT OF THE BATS!

When zombie hordes attack them in the game and bats invade their school in the real world, Ash, Morgan, and their friends realize that it's going to take all their talents to get to the bottom of these monstrous migrations.

978-1-9848-5048-5 (trade) — 978-1-9848-5050-8 (ebook) — 978-0-593-40123-1 (digital audio) — 978-1-9848-5049-2 (lib. bdg.)

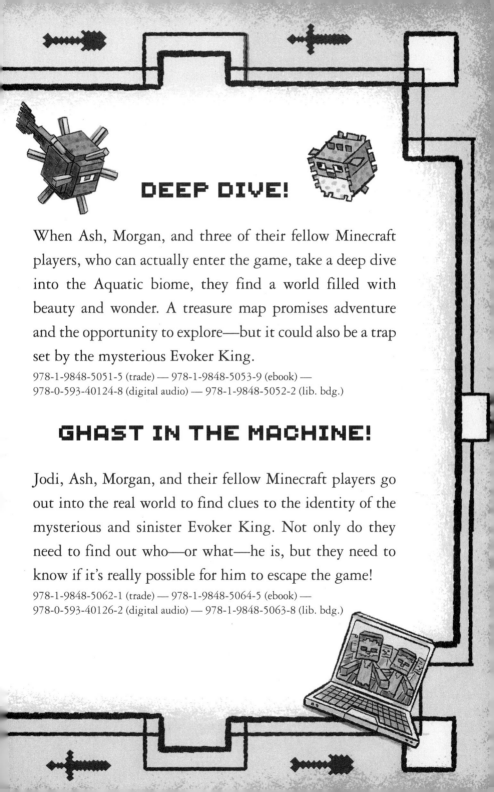

DEEP DIVE!

When Ash, Morgan, and three of their fellow Minecraft players, who can actually enter the game, take a deep dive into the Aquatic biome, they find a world filled with beauty and wonder. A treasure map promises adventure and the opportunity to explore—but it could also be a trap set by the mysterious Evoker King.

978-1-9848-5051-5 (trade) — 978-1-9848-5053-9 (ebook) —
978-0-593-40124-8 (digital audio) — 978-1-9848-5052-2 (lib. bdg.)

GHAST IN THE MACHINE!

Jodi, Ash, Morgan, and their fellow Minecraft players go out into the real world to find clues to the identity of the mysterious and sinister Evoker King. Not only do they need to find out who—or what—he is, but they need to know if it's really possible for him to escape the game!

978-1-9848-5062-1 (trade) — 978-1-9848-5064-5 (ebook) —
978-0-593-40126-2 (digital audio) — 978-1-9848-5063-8 (lib. bdg.)

DUNGEON CRAWL!

When Po, Morgan, and three of their fellow Minecraft players track the Evoker King to his home in the heart of a perilous dungeon, they have to gear up for an epic fantasy quest filled with danger, dragons, and hostile mobs.

978-1-9848-5065-2 (trade) — 978-1-9848-5067-6 (ebook) — 978-0-593-40128-6 (digital audio) — 978-1-9848-5066-9 (lib. bdg.)

LAST BLOCK STANDING!

As the world of Minecraft falls under the Evoker King's control, Morgan, Ash, and their friends get ready for the final showdown. But with their enemy now in possession of the most powerful building block in Minecraft, do they really stand a chance of defeating him?

978-1-9848-5069-0 (trade) — 978-1-9848-5071-3 (ebook) — 978-0-593-40130-9 (digital audio) — 978-1-9848-5070-6 (lib. bdg.)

THE ADVENTURES CONTINUE IN

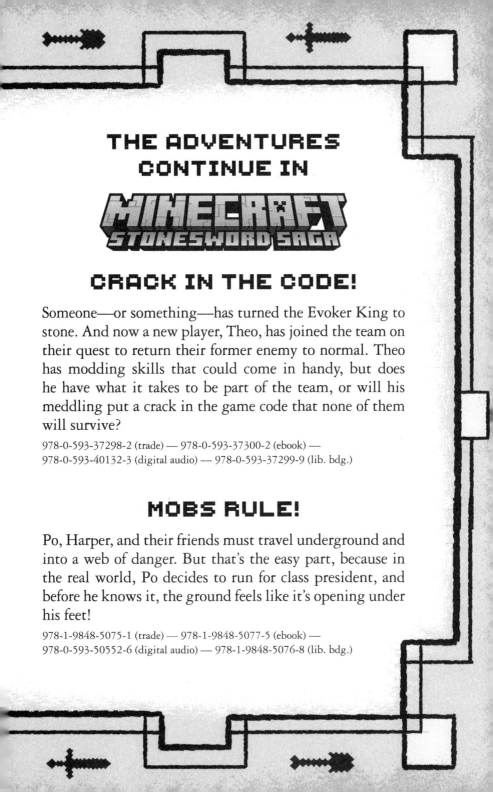

MINECRAFT
STONESWORD SAGA

CRACK IN THE CODE!

Someone—or something—has turned the Evoker King to stone. And now a new player, Theo, has joined the team on their quest to return their former enemy to normal. Theo has modding skills that could come in handy, but does he have what it takes to be part of the team, or will his meddling put a crack in the game code that none of them will survive?

978-0-593-37298-2 (trade) — 978-0-593-37300-2 (ebook) — 978-0-593-40132-3 (digital audio) — 978-0-593-37299-9 (lib. bdg.)

MOBS RULE!

Po, Harper, and their friends must travel underground and into a web of danger. But that's the easy part, because in the real world, Po decides to run for class president, and before he knows it, the ground feels like it's opening under his feet!

978-1-9848-5075-1 (trade) — 978-1-9848-5077-5 (ebook) — 978-0-593-50552-6 (digital audio) — 978-1-9848-5076-8 (lib. bdg.)

NEW PETS ON THE BLOCK!

When the third piece of the Evoker King takes the form of a Minecraft witch and sends Jodi, Morgan, and their friends on a quest to bring back an extremely rare animal mob, Jodi is determined to make sure that the mob stays safe no matter what!

978-1-9848-5094-2 (trade) — 978-1-9848-5096-6 (ebook) — 978-0-593-55978-9 (digital audio) — 978-1-9848-5095-9 (lib. bdg.)

TOO BEE, OR NOT TO BEE!

The bees around the school and the Stonesword Library are disappearing—and a splinter of the Evoker King has taken on the form of a bee colony with a hive mind! Could there be a connection? And to make matters worse, the rip in the Minecraft sky is growing bigger and darker.

978-0-593-56288-8 (trade) — 978-0-593-56290-1 (ebook) — 978-0-593-66817-7 (digital audio) — 978-0-593-56289-5 (lib. bdg.)

THE GOLEM'S GAME!

The next splinter of the Evoker King takes the form of a golem and challenges each member of the team to run a dangerous obstacle course. Forced to face the challenge alone, the team is not sure they are going to survive the golem's unwinnable game.

978-0-593-56291-8 (trade) — 978-0-593-56293-2 (ebook) — 978-0-593-68053-7 (digital audio) — 978-0-593-56292-5 (lib. bdg.)

MINECRAFT is a game about placing blocks and going on adventures. Build, play, and explore across infinitely generated worlds of mountains, caverns, oceans, jungles, and deserts. Defeat hordes of zombies, bake the cake of your dreams, venture to new dimensions, or build a skyscraper. What you do in Minecraft is up to you.

Nick Eliopulos is a writer who lives in Brooklyn (as many writers do). He likes to spend half his free time reading and the other half gaming. He cowrote the Adventurers Guild series with his best friend and works as a narrative designer for a small video game studio. After all these years, endermen still give him the creeps.

Alan Batson is a British cartoonist and illustrator. His works include *Everything I Need to Know I Learned from a Star Wars Little Golden Book, Everything That Glitters Is Guy!,* and *Spider-Ham.* Being extremely fond of cubes and travel to exotic places, he has recently begun to lend his talents to several different books on adventures in the world of Minecraft.

Chris Hill is an illustrator living in Birmingham, England, with his wife and two daughters and has been loving it for twenty-five years! When he's not working, he spends time with his family and trying to tire out his dog on long walks. If there's any time left after that, he loves to go riding on his motorcycle, feeling the wind on his face while contemplating his next illustration adventure.

JOURNEY INTO THE WORLD OF MINECRAFT

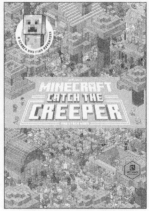

 rhcbooks.com

1481d

© 2023 Mojang AB. Minecraft, the Minecraft logo, the Mojang Studios logo and the Creeper logo are trademarks of Microsoft Corporation.